Young Learner's

Chippy Returns the Money

Sangita Koushik

Chippy the squirrel, lived with her mother. She always helped her mother with the housework.

One day, mother said to Chippy, "Dear, please go to the bakery and buy us a fresh loaf of bread for lunch."

So, Chippy went to the bakery. She wished the owner, "Good morning, Mr. Dill! Please give me a loaf of bread."

Mr. Dill smiled and replied, "Good morning, Chippy! I baked a special bread today. I am sure you will love it."

Chippy paid him for the bread. Mr. Dill took the money and gave her the balance amount.

Chippy thanked Mr. Dill and left. On the way back home, she counted the money.

She found that Mr. Dill had given her extra change. At first, Chippy was very happy.

She thought, "I have got extra money. I can buy some chocolates or cookies for myself!"

But, the next moment, she felt guilty. She realised, "It is not good to cheat. I cannot keep this extra money."

So, with this thought, Chippy walked back to the bakery. Mr. Dill was seeing a customer off at the door.

Mr. Dill saw Chippy and asked her, "What happened? Do you need something else?" Chippy replied, "Mr. Dill, you gave me extra change. Here, take it back." Mr. Dill was very happy with Chippy's honesty.

BAKERY

Mr. Dill patted Chippy on the back and said, "Thanks Chippy! Good girl! Here is your reward for being honest." He gave her a big chocolate.

Chippy was very happy. She had been honest. She had also earned a reward for it. She left the bakery happily and headed home.

Once home, Chippy told her mother everything. Mother gave her a tight hug. She said, "I am so proud of you Chippy. Well done, my child!"

Yes, well done, Chippy!

Moral: Honesty is the best policy.

Printed in India